# THE TREASURE OF TARTARY

BY

ROBERT E. HOWARD

**British Library Cataloguing-in-Publication Data**
A catalogue record for this book is available from the
British Library

# Contents

# Robert E. Howard

Robert Ervin Howard was born in Peaster, Texas in 1906. During his youth, his family moved between a variety of Texan boomtowns, and Howard – a bookish and somewhat introverted child – was steeped in the violent myths and legends of the Old South. Although he loved reading and learning, Howard developed a distinctly Texan, hardboiled outlook on the world. He became a passionate fan of boxing, taking it up at an amateur level, and from the age of nine began to write adventure tales of semi-historical bloodshed. In 1919, when Howard was thirteen, his family moved to the Central Texas hamlet of Cross Plains, where he would stay for the rest of his life.

At fifteen Howard began to read the pulp magazines of the day, and to write more seriously. The December 1922 issue of his high school newspaper featured two of his stories, 'Golden Hope Christmas' and 'West is West'. In 1924 he sold his first piece – a short caveman tale titled 'Spear and Fang' – for $16 to the not-yet-famous *Weird Tales* magazine. He published with the magazine regularly over the next few years. 1929 was a breakout year for Howard, in that the 23-year-old writer began to sell to other magazines, such as *Ghost Stories* and *Argosy*, both of whom had previously sent him hundreds of rejection slips. In 1930, he began a correspondence with weird fiction master H. P. Lovecraft which ran up to his death six years later, and is regarded as one of the great correspondence cycles in all of fantasy literature.

It was partly due to Lovecraft's encouragement that Howard created his most famous character, Conan the Cimmerian. Conan – a barbarian-turned-King during the Hyborian Age, a mythical period of some 12,000 years ago – featured in seventeen *Weird Tales* stories between 1933 and 1936, and is now regarded as having spawned the 'sword and sorcery' genre, making Howard's influence on fantasy literature comparable to that of J. R. R. Tolkien's. The Conan stories have since been adapted many times, most famously in the series of films starring Arnold Schwarzenegger.

Howard was enjoying an all-time high in sales by the beginning of 1936, but he was also deeply upset by the ill health of his mother, who had fallen into a coma. On the morning of June 11, 1936, he asked an attending nurse whether she would ever recover, and the nurse replied negatively. Howard walked to his car, parked outside the family home in Cross Plains, and shot himself. He died eight hours later, aged just thirty.

# CHAPTER 1: KEY TO THE TREASURE

It was not mere impulsiveness that sent Kirby O'Donnell into the welter of writhing limbs and whickering blades that loomed so suddenly in the semidarkness ahead of him. In that dark alley of Forbidden Shahrazar it was no light act to plunge headlong into a nameless brawl; and O'Donnell, for all his Irish love of a fight, was not disposed thoughtlessly to jeopardize his secret mission.

But the glimpse of a scarred, bearded face swept from his mind all thought and emotion save a crimson wave of fury. He acted instinctively.

Full into the midst of the flailing group, half-seen by the light of a distant cresset, O'Donnell leaped, kindhjal in hand. He was dimly aware that one man was fighting three or four others, but all his attention was fixed on a single tall gaunt form, dim in the shadows. His long, narrow, curved blade licked venomously at this figure, ploughing through cloth, bringing a yelp as the edge sliced skin. Something crashed down on O'Donnell's head, gun butt or bludgeon, and he reeled, and closed with someone he could not see.

His groping hand locked on a chain that encircled a bull neck, and with a straining gasp he ripped upward and felt his keen kindhjal slice through cloth, skin and belly muscles. An agonized groan burst from his victim's lips, and blood gushed sickeningly over O'Donnell's hand.

Through a blur of clearing sight, the American saw a broad bearded face falling away from him--not the face he had seen before. The next instant he had leaped clear of the dying man, and was slashing at the shadowy forms about him. An instant of flickering steel, and then the figures were running fleetly up the alley. O'Donnell, springing in pursuit, his hot blood lashed to murderous fury, tripped over a writhing form and fell headlong. He rose, cursing, and was aware of a man near him, panting heavily. A tall man, with a long curved blade in hand. Three forms lay in the mud of the alley.

"Come, my friend, whoever you are!" the tall man panted in Turki. "They have fled, but they will return with others. Let us go!"

O'Donnell made no reply. Temporarily accepting the alliance into which chance had cast him, he followed the tall stranger who ran down the winding alley with the sure foot of familiarity. Silence held them until they emerged from a low dark arch, where a tangle of alleys debouched upon a broad square, vaguely lighted by small fires about which groups of turbaned men squabbled and brewed tea. A reek of unwashed bodies mingled with the odors of horses and camels. None noticed the two men standing in the shadow made by the angle of the mud wall.

O'Donnell looked at the stranger, seeing a tall slim man with thin dark features. Under his khalat which was draggled and darkly splashed, showed the silver-heeled boots of a horseman. His turban was awry, and though he had sheathed his scimitar, blood clotted the hilt and the scabbard mouth.

The keen black eyes took in every detail of the American's appearance, but O'Donnell did not flinch. His disguise had stood the test too many times for him to doubt its effectiveness.

The American was somewhat above medium height, leanly built, but with broad shoulders and corded sinews which gave him a strength out of all proportion to his weight. He was a hard-woven mass of wiry muscles and steel string nerves, combining the wolf-trap coordination of a natural fighter with a berserk fury resulting from an overflowing nervous energy. The kindhjal in his girdle and the scimitar at his hip were as much a part of him as his hands.

He wore the Kurdish boots, vest and girdled khalat like a man born to them. His keen features, bummed to bronze by desert suns, were almost as dark as those of his companion.

"Tell me thy name," requested the other. "I owe my life to thee."

"I am Ali el Ghazi, a Kurd," answered O'Donnell.

No hint of suspicion shadowed the other's countenance. Under the coiffed Arab kafiyeh O'Donnell's eyes blazed lambent blue, but blue eyes were not at all unknown among the warriors of the Iranian highlands.

The Turk lightly and swiftly touched the hawk-headed pommel of O'Donnell's scimitar.

"I will not forget," he promised. "I will know thee wherever we meet again. Now it were best we separated and went far from this spot, for men with knives will be seeking me--and thou too, for aiding me." And like a shadow he glided among the camels and bales and was gone.

O'Donnell stood silently for an instant, one ear cocked back toward the alley, the other absently taking in the sounds of the night. Somewhere a thin wailing voice sang to a twanging native lute. Somewhere else a feline-like burst of profanity marked the progress of a quarrel. O'Donnell breathed deep with contentment, despite the grim Hooded Figure that stalked forever at his shoulder, and the recent rage that still seethed in his veins. This was the real heart of the East, the East which had long ago stolen his heart and led him to wander afar from his own people.

He realized that he still gripped something in his left hand, and he lifted it to the flickering light of a nearby fire. It was a length of gold chain, one of its massy links twisted and broken. From it depended a curious plaque of beaten gold, somewhat larger than a silver dollar, but oval rather than round. There was no ornament, only a boldly carven inscription which O'Donnell, with all his Eastern lore, could not decipher.

He knew that he had torn the chain from the neck of the man he had killed in that black alley, but he had no idea as to its meaning. Slipping it into his broad girdle, he strode across the square, walking with the swagger of a nomadic horseman that was so natural to him.

Leaving the square he strode down a narrow street, the overhanging balconies of which almost touched one another. It was not late. Merchants in flowing silk robes sat cross-legged before their booths, extolling the quality of their goods--Mosul silk, matchlocks from Herat, edged weapons from India, and seed pearls from Baluchistan, hawk-like Afghans and weapon-girdled Uzbeks jostled him. Lights streamed through silk-covered windows overhead, and the light silvery laughter of women rose above the noise of barter and dispute.

There was a tingle in the realization that he, Kirby O'Donnell, was the first Westerner ever to set foot in forbidden Shahrazar, tucked away in a nameless valley not many days' journey from where the Afghan mountains swept down into the steppes of the Turkomans. As a wandering Kurd, traveling with a caravan from Kabul he had come, staking his life against the golden lure of a treasure beyond men's dreams.

In the bazaars and serais he had heard a tale: To Shaibar Khan, the Uzbek chief who had made himself master of Shahrazar, the city had given up its ancient secret. The Uzbek had found the treasure hidden there so long ago by Muhammad Shah, king of Khuwarezm, the Land of the Throne of Gold, when his empire fell before the Mongols.

O'Donnell was in Shahrazar to steal that treasure; and he did not change his plans because of the bearded face he had recognized in the alley--the face of an old and hated enemy. Yar Akbar the Afridi, traitor and murderer.

O'Donnell turned from the street and entered a narrow arched gate which stood open as if in invitation. A narrow stair went up from a small court to a balcony. This he mounted, guided by the tinkle of a guitar and a plaintive voice singing in Pushtu.

He entered a room whose latticed casement overhung the street, and the singer ceased her song to greet him and make half-mocking salaam with a lithe flexing of supple limbs. He replied, and deposited himself on a divan. The furnishings of the room were not elaborate, but they were costly. The garments of the woman who watched interestedly were of silk, her satin vest sewn with seed pearls. Her dark eyes, over the filmy yasmaq, were lustrous and expressive, the eyes of a Persian.

"Would my lord have food--and wine?" she inquired; and O'Donnell signified assent with the lordly gesture of a Kurdish swashbuckler who is careful not to seem too courteous to any woman, however famed in intrigue she may be. He had come there not for food and drink, but because he had heard in the bazaars that news of many kinds blew on the winds through the house of Ayisha, where men from far and near came to drink her wine and listen to her songs.

She served him, and, sinking down on cushions near him, watched him eat and drink. O'Donnell's appetite was not feigned. Many lean days had taught him to eat when and where he could. Ayisha seemed to him more like a curious child than an intriguing woman, evincing so much interest over a wandering Kurd, but he knew that she was weighing him carefully behind her guileless stare, as she weighed all men who came into her house.

In that hotbed of plot and ambitions, the wandering stranger today might be the Amir of Afghanistan or the Shah of Persia tomorrow--or the morrow might see his headless body dangling as a feast for the birds.

"You have a good sword," said she. He involuntarily touched the hilt. It was an Arab blade, long, lean, curved like the crescent moon, with a brass hawk's head for a pommel.

"It has cut many a Turkoman out of the saddle," he boasted, with his mouth full, carrying out his character. Yet it was no empty boast.

"Hai!" She believed him and was impressed. She rested her chin on her small fists and gazed up at him, as if his dark, hawk-like face had caught her fancy.

"The Khan needs swords like yours," she said.

"The Khan has many swords," he retorted, gulping wine loudly.

"No more than he will need if Orkhan Bahadur comes against him," she prophesied.

"I have heard of this Orkhan," he replied. And so he had; who in Central Asia had not heard of the daring and valorous Turkoman chief who defied the power of Moscow and had cut to pieces a Russian expedition sent to subdue him? "In the bazaars they say the Khan fears him."

That was a blind venture. Men did not speak of Shaibar Khan's fears openly.

Ayisha laughed. "Who does the Khan fear? Once the Amir sent troops to take Shahrazar, and those who lived were glad to flee! Yet if any man lives who could storm the city, Orkhan Bahadur is that man. Only tonight the Uzbeks were hunting his spies through the alleys."

O'Donnell remembered the Turkish accent of the stranger he had unwittingly aided. It was quite possible that the man was a Turkoman spy.

As he pondered this, Ayisha's sharp eyes discovered the broken end of the gold chain dangling from his girdle, and with a gurgle of delight she snatched it forth before he could stop her. Then with a squeal she dropped it as if it were hot, and prostrated herself in wriggling abasement among the cushions.

He scowled and picked up the trinket.

"Woman, what are you about?" he demanded.

"Your pardon, lord!" She clasped her hands, but her fear seemed more feigned than real; her eyes sparkled. "I did not know it was the token. Aie, you have been making game of me--asking me things none could know better than yourself. Which of the Twelve are you?"

"You babble as bees hum!" He scowled, dangling the pendant before her eyes. "You speak as one of knowledge, when, by Allah, you know not the meaning of this thing."

"Nay, but I do!" she protested. "I have seen such emblems before on the breasts of the emirs of the Inner Chamber. I know that it is a talsmin greater than the seal of the Amir, and the wearer comes and goes at will in or out of the Shining Palace."

"But why, wench, why?" he growled impatiently.

"Nay, I will whisper what you know so well," she answered, kneeling beside him. Her breath came soft as the sighing of the distant night wind. "It is the symbol of a Guardian of the Treasure!"

She fell away from him laughing. "Have I not spoken truly?"

He did not at once reply. His brain was dizzy, the blood pounding madly in his veins.

"Say nothing of this," he said at last, rising. "Your life upon it." And casting her a handful of coins at random, he hurried down the stair and into the street. He realized that his departure was too abrupt, but he was too dizzy, with the realization of what had fallen into his hands, for an entirely placid course of action.

The treasure! In his hand he held what well might be the key to it--at least a key into the palace, to gain entrance into which he had racked his brain in vain ever since coming to Shahrazar. His visit to Ayisha had borne fruit beyond his wildest dreams.

# CHAPTER 2: THE UNHOLY PLAN

Doubtless in Muhammad Shah's day the Shining Palace deserved its name; even now it preserved some of its former splendor. It was separated from the rest of the city by a thick wall, and at the great gate there always stood a guard of Uzbeks with Lee-Enfield rifles, and girdles bristling with knives and pistols.

Shaibar Khan had an almost superstitious terror of accidental gunfire, and would allow only edged weapons to be brought into the palace. But his warriors were armed with the best rifles that could be smuggled into the hills.

There was a limit to O'Donnell's audacity. There might be men on guard at the main gates who knew by sight all the emirs of the symbol. He made his way to a small side gate, through a loophole in which, at his imperious call, there peered a black man with the wizened features of a mute. O'Donnell had fastened the broken finks together and the chain now looped his corded neck. He indicated the plaque which rested on the silk of his khalat; and with a deep salaam, the black man opened the gate.

O'Donnell drew a deep breath. He was in the heart of the lion's lair now, and he dared not hesitate or pause to deliberate. He found himself in a garden which gave onto an open court surrounded by arches supported on marble pillars. He crossed the court, meeting no one. On the opposite side a grim-looking Uzbek, leaning on a spear, scanned him narrowly but said nothing. O'Donnell's skin crawled as he strode past the somber warrior, but the man merely stared curiously at the gold oval gleaming against the Kurdish vest.

O'Donnell found himself in a corridor whose walls were decorated by a gold frieze, and he went boldly on, seeing only soft-footed slaves who took no heed of him. As he passed into another corridor, broader and hung with velvet tapestries, his heart leaped into his mouth.

It was a tall slender man in long fur-trimmed robes and a silk turban who glided from an arched doorway and halted him. The man had the pale oval face of a Persian, with a black pointed beard, and dark shadowed eyes. As with the others his gaze sought first the talsmin on O'Donnell's breast--the token, undoubtedly, of a servitor beyond suspicion.

"Come with me!" snapped the Persian. "I have work for you." And vouchsafing no further enlightenment, he stalked down the corridor as if expecting O'Donnell to follow without question; which, indeed, the American did, believing that such would have been the action of the genuine Guardian of the Treasure. He knew this Persian was Ahmed Pasha, Shaibar Khan's vizir; he had seen him riding along the streets with the royal house troops.

The Persian led the way into a small domed chamber, without windows, the walls hung with thick tapestries. A small bronze lamp lighted it dimly. Ahmed Pasha drew aside the hangings, directly behind a heap of cushions, and disclosed a hidden alcove.

"Stand there with drawn sword," he directed. Then he hesitated. "Can you speak or understand any Frankish tongue?" he demanded. The false Kurd shook his head.

"Good!" snapped Ahmed Pasha. "You are here to watch, not to listen. Our lord does not trust the man he is to meet here--alone. You are stationed behind the spot where this man will sit. Watch him like a hawk. If he makes a move against the Khan, cleave his skull. If harm comes to our prince, you shall be flayed alive." He paused, glared an instant, then snarled:

"And hide that emblem, fool! Shall the whole world know you are an emir of the Treasure?"

"Hearkening and obedience, ya khawand," mumbled O'Donnell, thrusting the symbol inside his garments. Ahmed jerked the tapestries together, and left the chamber. O'Donnell glanced through a tiny opening, waiting for the soft pad of the vizir's steps to fade away before he should glide out and take up again his hunt for the treasure.

But before he could move, there was a low mutter of voices, and two men entered the chamber from opposite sides. One bowed low and did not venture to seat himself until the other had deposited his fat body on the cushions, and indicated permission.

O'Donnell knew that he looked on Shaibar Khan, once the terror of the Kirghiz steppes, and now lord of Shahrazar. The Uzbek had the broad powerful build of his race, but his thick limbs were soft from easy living. His eyes held some of their old restless fire, but the muscles of his face seemed flabby, and his features were lined and purpled with debauchery. And there seemed something else--a worried, haunted look, strange in that son of reckless nomads. O'Donnell wondered if the possession of the treasure was weighing on his mind.

The other man was slender, dark, his garments plain beside the gorgeous ermine-trimmed kaftan, pearl-sewn girdle and green, emerald-crested turban of the Khan.

This stranger plunged at once into conversation, low voiced but animated and urgent. He did most of the talking, while Shaibar Khan listened, occasionally interjecting a question, or a grunt of gratification. The Khan's weary eyes began to blaze, and his pudgy hands knotted as if they gripped again the hilt of the blade which had carved his way to power.

And Kirby O'Donnell forgot to curse the luck which held him prisoner while precious time drifted by. Both men spoke a tongue the American had not heard in years--a European language. And scanning closely the slim dark stranger, O'Donnell admitted himself baffled. If the man

16

were, as he suspected, a European disguised as an Oriental, then O'Donnell knew he had met his equal in masquerade.

For it was European politics he talked, European politics that lay behind the intrigues of the East. He spoke of war and conquest, and vast hordes rolling down the Khybar Pass into India; to complete the overthrow, said the dark slender man, of a rule outworn.

He promised power and honors to Shaibar Khan, and O'Donnell, listening, realized that the Uzbek was but a pawn in his game, no less than those others he mentioned. The Khan, narrow of vision, saw only a mountain kingdom for himself, reaching down into the plains of Persia and India, and backed by European guns--not realizing those same guns could just as easily overwhelm him when the time was ripe.

But O'Donnell, with his western wisdom, read behind the dark stranger's words, and recognized there a plan of imperial dimensions, and the plot of a European power to seize half of Asia. And the first move in that game was to be the gathering of warriors by Shaibar Khan. How? With the treasure of Khuwarezm! With it he could buy all the swords of Central Asia.

So the dark man talked and the Uzbek listened like an old wolf who harks to the trampling of the musk oxen in the snow. O'Donnell listened, his blood freezing as the dark man casually spoke of invasions and massacres; and as the plot progressed and became more plain in detail, more monstrous and ruthless in conception, he trembled with a mad urge to leap from his cover and slash and hack both these bloody devils into pieces with the scimitar that quivered in his nervous grasp. Only a sense of self-preservation stayed him from this madness; and presently Shaibar Khan concluded the audience and left the chamber, followed by the dark stranger. O'Donnell saw this one smile furtively, like a man who has victory in his grasp.

O'Donnell started to draw aside the curtain, when Ahmed Pasha came padding into the chamber. It occurred to the American that it would be better to let the vizir find him at his post. But before Ahmed could speak, or draw aside the curtain, there sounded a rapid pattering of bare feet in the corridor outside, and a man burst into the room, wild eyed and panting. At the sight of him a red mist wavered across O'Donnell's sight. It was Yar Akbar!

# CHAPTER 3: WOLF PACK

The Afridi fell on his knees before Ahmed Pasha. His garments were tattered; blood seeped from a broken tooth and clotted his straggly beard.

"Oh, master," he panted, "the dog has escaped!"

"Escaped!" The vizir rose to his full height, his face convulsed with passion. O'Donnell thought that he would strike down the Afridi, but his arm quivered, fell by his side.

"Speak!" The Persian's voice was dangerous as the hiss of a cobra.

"We hedged him in a dark alley," Yar Akbar babbled. "He fought like Shaitan. Then others came to his aid--a whole nest of Turkomans, we thought, but mayhap it was but one man. He too was a devil! He slashed my side--see the blood! For hours since we have hunted them, but found no trace. He is over the wall and gone!" In his agitation Yar Akbar plucked at a chain about his neck; from it depended an oval like that held by O'Donnell. The American realized that Yar Akbar, too, was an emir of the Treasure. The Afridi's eyes burned like a wolf's in the gloom, and his voice sank.

"He who wounded me slew Othman," he whispered fearfully, "and despoiled him of the talsmin!"

"Dog!" The vizir's blow knocked the Afridi sprawling. Ahmed Pasha was livid. "Call the other emirs of the Inner Chamber, swiftly!"

Yar Akbar hastened into the corridor, and Ahmed Pasha called:

"Ohe! You who hide behind the hangings--come forth!" There was no reply, and pale with sudden suspicion, Ahmed drew a curved dagger and with a pantherish spring tore the tapestry aside. The alcove was empty.

As he glared in bewilderment, Yar Akbar ushered into the chamber as unsavory a troop of ruffians as a man might meet, even in the hills: Uzbeks, Afghans, Gilzais, Pathans, scarred with crime and old in wickedness. Ahmed Pasha counted them swiftly. With Yar Akbar there were eleven.

"Eleven," he muttered. "And dead Othman makes twelve. All these men are known to you, Yar Akbar?"

"My head on it!" swore the Afridi. "These be all true men."

Ahmed clutched his beard.

"Then, by God, the One True God," he groaned, "that Kurd I set to guard the Khan was a spy and a traitor." And at that moment a shriek and a clash of steel re-echoed through the palace.

When O'Donnell heard Yar Akbar gasping out his tale to the vizir, he knew the game was up. He did not believe that the alcove was a blind niche in the wall; and, running swift and practiced hands over the panels, he found and pressed a hidden catch. An instant before Ahmed Pasha tore aside the tapestry, the American wriggled his lean body through the opening and found himself in a dimly lighted chamber on the other side of the wall. A black slave dozed on his haunches, unmindful of the blade that hovered over his ebony neck, as O'Donnell glided across the room, and through a curtained doorway.

He found himself back in the corridor into which one door of the audience chamber opened, and crouching among the curtains, he saw Yar Akbar come up the hallway with his villainous crew. He saw, too, that they had come up a marble stair at the end of the hall.

His heart leaped. In that direction, undoubtedly, lay the treasure--now supposedly unguarded. As soon as the emirs vanished into the audience chamber where the vizir waited, O'Donnell ran swiftly and recklessly down the corridor.

But even as he reached the stairs, a man sitting on them sprang up, brandishing a tulwar. A black slave, evidently left there with definite orders, for the sight of the symbol on O'Donnell's breast did not halt him. O'Donnell took a desperate chance, gambling his speed against the cry that rose in the thick black throat.

He lost. His scimitar licked through the massive neck and the Soudani rolled down the stairs, spurting blood. But his yell had rung to the roof.

And at that yell the emirs of the gold came headlong out of the audience chamber, giving tongue like a pack of wolves. They did not need Ahmed's infuriated shriek of recognition and command. They were men picked for celerity of action as well as courage, and it seemed to O'Donnell that they were upon him before the Negro's death yell had ceased to echo.

He met the first attacker, a hairy Pathan, with a long lunge that sent his scimitar point through the thick throat even as the man's broad tulwar went up for a stroke. Then a tall Uzbek swung his heavy blade like a butcher's cleaver. No time to parry; O'Donnell caught the stroke near his own hilt, and his knees bent under the impact.

But the next instant the kindhjal in his left hand ripped through the Uzbek's entrails, and with a powerful heave of his whole body, O'Donnell hurled the dying man against those behind him, bearing them back with him. Then O'Donnell wheeled and ran, his eyes blazing defiance of the death that whickered at his back.

Ahead of him another stair led up. O'Donnell reached it one long bound ahead of his pursuers, gained the steps and wheeled, all in one motion, slashing down at the heads of the pack that came clamoring after him.

Shaibar Khan's broad pale face peered up at the melee from the curtains of an archway, and O'Donnell was grateful to the Khan's obsessional fear that had barred firearms from the palace. Otherwise, he would already have been shot down like a dog. He himself had no gun; the pistol with which he had started the adventure had slipped from its holster somewhere on that long journey, and lay lost among the snows of the Himalayas.

No matter; he had never yet met his match with cold steel. But no blade could long have held off the ever-increasing horde that swarmed up the stair at him.

He had the advantage of position, and they could not crowd past him on the narrow stair; their very numbers hindered them. His flesh crawled with the fear that others would come down the stair and take him from behind, but none came. He retreated slowly, plying his dripping blades with berserk frenzy. A steady stream of taunts and curses flowed from his lips, but even in his fury he spoke in the tongues of the East, and not one of his assailants realized that the madman who opposed them was anything but a Kurd.

He was bleeding from a dozen flesh cuts, when he reached the head of the stairs which ended in an open trap. Simultaneously the wolves below him came clambering up to drag him down. One gripped his knees, another was hewing madly at his head. The others howled below them, unable to get at their prey.

O'Donnell stooped beneath the sweep of a tulwar and his scimitar split the skull of the wielder. His kindhjal he drove through the breast of the man who clung to his knees, and kicking the clinging body away from him, he reeled up through the trap. With frantic energy, he gripped the heavy iron-bound door and slammed it down, falling across it in semicollapse.

The splintering of wood beneath him warned him and he rolled clear just as a steel point crunched up through the door and quivered in the starlight. He found and shot the bolt, and then lay prostrate, panting for breath. How long the heavy wood would resist the attacks from below he did not know.

He was on a flat-topped roof, the highest part of the palace. Rising, he stumbled over to the nearest parapet, and looked down, onto lower roofs. He saw no way to get down. He was trapped.

It was the darkness just before dawn. He was on a higher level than the walls or any of the other houses in Shahrazar. He could dimly make out the sheer of the great cliffs which flanked the valley in which Shahrazar stood, and he saw the starlight's pale glimmer on the slim river which trickled past the massive walls. The valley ran southeast and northwest.

And suddenly the wind, whispering down from the north, brought a burst of crackling reports. Shots? He stared northwestward, toward where, he knew, the valley pitched upward, narrowing to a sheer gut, and a mud-walled village dominated the pass. He saw a dull red glow against the sky. Again came reverberations.

Somewhere in the streets below sounded a frantic clatter of flying hoofs that halted before the palace gate. There was silence then, in which O'Donnell heard the splintering blows on the trap door, and the heavy breathing of the men who struck them. Then suddenly they ceased as if the attackers had dropped dead; utter silence attended a shrilling voice, indistinct through distance and muffling walls. A wild clamor burst forth in the streets below; men shouted, women screamed.

No more blows fell on the trap. Instead there were noises below--the rattle of arms, tramp of men, and a voice that held a note of hysteria shouting orders.

O'Donnell heard the clatter of galloping horses, and saw torches moving through the streets, toward the northwestern gate. In the darkness up the valley he saw orange jets of flame and heard the unmistakable reports of firearms.

Shrugging his shoulders, he sat down in an angle of the parapet, his scimitar across his knees. And there weary Nature asserted itself, and in spite of the clamor below him, and the riot in his blood, he slept.

# CHAPTER 4: FURIOUS BATTLE

He did not sleep long, for dawn was just stealing whitely over the mountains when he awoke. Rifles were cracking all around, and crouching at the parapet, he saw the reason. Shahrazar was besieged by warriors in sheepskin coats and fur kalpaks. Herds of their horses grazed just beyond rifle fire, and the warriors themselves were firing from every rock and tree. Numbers of them were squirming along the half-dry river bed, among the willows, sniping at the men on the walls, who gave back their fire.

The Turkomans of Orkhan Bahadur! That blaze in the darkness told of the fate of the village that guarded the pass. Turks seldom made night raids; but Orkhan was nothing if not original.

The Uzbeks manned the walls, and O'Donnell believed he could make out the bulky shape and crested turban of Shaibar Khan among a cluster of peacock-clad nobles. And as he gazed at the turmoil in the streets below, the belief grew that every available Uzbek in the city was on the walls. This was no mere raid; it was a tribal war of extermination.

O'Donnell's Irish audacity rose like heady wine in his veins, and he tore aside the splintered door and gazed down the stairs. The bodies still lay on the steps, stiff and unseeing. No living human met his gaze as he stole down the stairs, scimitar in hand. He gained the broad corridor, and still he saw no one. He hurried down the stair whereon he had slain the black slave, and reached a broad chamber with a single tapestried door.

There was the sudden crash of a musket; a spurt of flame stabbed at him. The ball whined past him and he covered the space with a long leap, grappled a snarling, biting figure behind the tapestry and dragged it into the open. It was Ahmed Pasha.

"Accursed one!" The vizir fought like a mad dog. "I guessed you would come skulking here--Allah's curse on the hashish that has made my hand unsteady--"

His dagger girded through O'Donnell's garments, drawing blood. Under his silks the Persian's muscles were like taut wires. Employing his superior weight, the American hurled himself hard against the other, driving the vizir's head back against the stone wall with a stunning crack. As the Persian relaxed with a groan, O'Donnell's left hand wrenched from his grasp and lurched upward, and the keen kindhjal encountered flesh and bone.

The American lifted the still twitching corpse and thrust it behind the tapestry, hiding it as best he could. A bunch of keys at the dead man's girdle caught his attention, and they were in his hand as he approached the curtained door.

The heavy teakwood portal, bound in arabesqued copper, would have resisted any onslaught short of artillery.

A moment's fumbling with the massive keys, and O'Donnell found the right one. He passed into a narrow corridor dimly lighted by some obscure means. The walls were of marble, the floor of mosaics. It ended at what seemed to be a blank carven wall, until O'Donnell saw a thin crack in the marble.

Through carelessness or haste, the secret door had been left partly open. O'Donnell heard no sound, and was inclined to believe that Ahmed Pasha had remained to guard the treasure alone. He gave the vizir credit for wit and courage.

O'Donnell pulled open the door--a wide block of marble revolving on a pivot--and halted short, a low cry escaping his lips. He had come full upon the treasure of Khuwarezm, and the sight stunned him!

The dim light must have come through hidden interstices in the colored dome of the circular chamber in which he stood. It illumined a shining pyramidal heap upon a dais in the center of the floor, a platform that was a great round slab of pure jade. And on that jade gleamed tokens of wealth beyond the dreams of madness. The foundations of the pile consisted of blocks of virgin gold and upon them lay, rising to a pinnacle of blazing splendor, ingots of hammered silver, ornaments of golden enamel, wedges of jade, pearls of incredible perfection, inlaid ivory, diamonds that dazzled the sight, rubies like clotted blood, emeralds like drops of green fire, pulsing sapphires--O'Donnell's senses refused to accept the wonder of what he saw. Here, indeed, was wealth sufficient to buy every sword in Asia. A sudden sound brought him about. Someone was coming down the corridor outside, someone who labored for breath and ran staggeringly. A quick glance around, and O'Donnell slipped behind the rich gilt-worked arras which masked the walls. A niche where, perhaps, had stood an idol in the old pagan days, admitted his lean body, and he gazed through a slit cut in the velvet.

It was Shaibar Khan who came into the chamber. The Khan's garments were torn and splashed darkly. He stared at his treasure with haunted eyes, and he groaned. Then he called for Ahmed Pasha.

One man came, but it was not the vizir who lay dead in the outer corridor. It was Yar Akbar, crouching like a great gray wolf, beard bristling in his perpetual snarl.

"Why was the treasure left unguarded?" demanded Shaibar Khan petulantly. "Where is Ahmed Pasha?"

"He sent us on the wall," answered Yar Akbar, hunching his shoulders in servile abasement. "He said he would guard the treasure himself."

"No matter!" Shaibar Khan was shaking like a man with an ague. "We are lost. The people have risen against me and opened the gates to that devil Orkhan Bahadur. His Turkomans are cutting down my Uzbeks in the streets. But he shall not have the treasure. See ye that golden bar that juts from the wall, like a sword hilt from the scabbard? I have but to pull that, and the treasure falls into the subterranean river which runs below this palace, to be lost forever to the sight of men. Yar Akbar, I give you a last command--pull that bar!"

Yar Akbar moaned and wrung his beard, but his eyes were red as a wolf's, and he turned his ear continually toward the outer door.

"Nay, lord, ask of me anything but that!"

"Then I will do it!" Shaibar Khan moved toward the bar, reached out his hand to grasp it. With a snarl of a wild beast, Yar Akbar sprang on his back, grunting as he struck. O'Donnell saw the point of the Khyber knife spring out of Shaibar Khan's silk-clad breast, as the Uzbek chief threw wide his arms, cried out chokingly, and tumbled forward to the floor. Yar Akbar spurned the dying body with a vicious foot.

"Fool!" he croaked. "I will buy my life from Orkhan Bahadur. Aye, this treasure shall gain me much honor with him, now the other emirs are dead--"

He halted, crouching and glaring, the reddened knife quivering in his hairy fist. O'Donnell had swept aside the tapestry and stepped into the open. "Y'Allah!" ejaculated the Afridi. "The dog-Kurd!"

"Look more closely, Yar Akbar," answered O'Donnell grimly, throwing back his kafiyeh and speaking in English.

"Do you not remember the Gorge of Izz ed din and the scout trapped there by your treachery? One man escaped, you dog of the Khyber."

Slowly a red flame grew in Yar Akbar's eyes.

"El Shirkuh!" he muttered, giving O'Donnell his Afghan name--the Mountain Lion. Then, with a howl that rang to the domed roof, he launched himself through the air, his three-foot knife gleaming.

O'Donnell did not move his feet. A supple twist of his torso avoided the thrust, and the furiously driven knife hissed between left arm and body, tearing his khalat. At the same instant O'Donnell's left forearm bent up and under the lunging arm that guided the knife. Yar Akbar screamed, spat on the kindhjal's narrow blade. Unable to halt his headlong rush, he caromed bodily against O'Donnell, bearing him down.

They struck the floor together, and Yar Akbar, with a foot of trenchant steel in his vitals, yet reared up, caught O'Donnell's hair in a fierce grasp, gasped a curse, lifted his knife--and then his wild beast vitality failed him, and with a convulsive shudder he rolled clear and lay still in a spreading pool of blood.

O'Donnell rose and stared down at the bodies upon the floor, then at the glittering heap on the jade slab. His soul yearned to it with the fierce yearning that had haunted him for years. Dared he take the desperate chance of hiding it under the very noses of the invading Turkomans? If he could, he might escape, to return later, and bear it away. He had taken more desperate chances before.

Across his mental vision flashed a picture of a slim dark stranger who spoke a European tongue. It was lure of the treasure which had led Orkhan Bahadur out of his steppes; and the treasure in his hands would be as dangerous as it was in the hands of Shaibar Khan. The Power represented by the dark stranger could deal with the Turkoman as easily as with the Uzbek.

No; one Oriental adventurer with that treasure was as dangerous to the peace of Asia as another. He dared not run the risk of Orkhan Bahadur finding that pile of gleaming wealth--sweat suddenly broke out on O'Donnell's body as he realized, for once in his life, a driving power mightier than his own desire. The helpless millions of India were in his mind as, cursing sickly, he gripped the gold bar and heaved it!

With a grinding boom something gave way, the jade slab moved, turned, tilted, and disappeared, and with it vanished, in a final iridescent burst of dazzling splendor, the treasure of Khuwarezm. Far below came a sullen splash, and the sound of waters roaring in the darkness; then silence, and where a black hole had gaped there showed a circular slab of the same substance as the rest of the floor.

O'Donnell hurried from the chamber. He did not wish to be found where the Turkomans might connect him with the vanishing of the treasure they had battled to win. Let them think, if thcy would, that Shaibar Khan and Yar Akbar had disposed of it somehow, and slain one another. As he emerged from the palace into an outer court, lean warriors in sheepskin kaftans and high fur caps were swarming in. Cartridge belts crossed on their breasts, and yataghans hung at their girdles. One of them lifted a rifle and took deliberate aim at O'Donnell.

Then it was struck aside, and a voice shouted:

"By Allah, it is my friend Ali el Ghazi!" There strode forward a tall man whose kalpak was of white lambskin, and whose kaftan was trimmed with ermine. O'Donnell recognized the man he had aided in the alley.

"I am Orkhan Bahadur!" exclaimed the chief with a ringing laugh. "Put up your sword, friend; Shahrazar is mine! The heads of the Uzbeks are heaped in the market square! When I fled from their swords last night, they little guessed my warriors awaited my coming in the mountains beyond the pass! Now I am prince of Shahrazar, and thou art my cup-companion. Ask what thou wilt, yea, even a share of the treasure of Khuwarezm--when we find it."

"When you find it!" O'Donnell mentally echoed, sheathing his scimitar with a Kurdish swagger. The American was something of a fatalist. He had come out of this adventure with his life at least, and the rest was in the hands of Allah.

"Alhamdolillah!" said O'Donnell, joining arms with his new cup-companion.

THE END